SNUG A A BUG!

Scenes from family life

Collected by Gwenda Beed Davey
Illustrated by Peter Viska

Melbourne
Oxford University Press
Oxford   Auckland   New York

OXFORD UNIVERSITY PRESS

Oxford New York Toronto
Delhi Bombay Calcutta Madras Karachi
Petaling Jaya Singapore Hong Kong Tokyo
Nairobi Dar es Salaam Cape Town
Melbourne Auckland
and associated companies in
Berlin Ibadan

OXFORD is a trade mark of Oxford University Press

© Text Gwenda Beed Davey 1990
© Illustrations Peter Viska 1990
First published 1990
Reprinted 1990, 1992

This book is copyright. Apart from any fair dealing for the purposes of private study, research, criticism or review as permitted under the Copyright Act, no part may be reproduced, stored in a retrieval system, or transmitted, in any form or by any means electronic, mechanical, photocopying, recording, or otherwise without prior written permission. Inquiries to be made to Oxford University Press.

National Library of Australia
Cataloguing-in-Publication data:

Snug as a bug

Includes index.
ISBN 0 19 553036 5.

1. Folk literature, Australian. 2. Proverbs, Australia. 3. Nursery rhymes, English.
I. Davey, Gwenda. II. Viska, Peter.

398.20994

Typeset by Bookset, Melbourne
Printed in Australia by Impact Printing Victoria Pty Ltd
Published by Oxford University Press,
253 Normanby Road, South Melbourne, Australia

Contents

Tea-Time   3

Curiosity   41

Silly Sayings   69

Ifs and Don'ts   83

Bed-Time   97

Index   104

Acknowledgements

My thanks go to my former students at Footscray Institute of Technology and the Institute of Early Childhood Development (now School of Early Childhood Studies, University of Melbourne), and to Tim Bowden and the ABC's Social History Unit, for their help in preparing this book.

Introduction

Snug As A Bug! is a collection of family sayings and rhymes which loving and exasperated adults use with their children. All the sayings have been collected in Australia, and most are in widespread use today.

Snug As A Bug! has been prepared as a companion volume to June Factor's collections of children's chants and rhymes — *Far Out, Brussel Sprout!*, *All Right, Vegemite!*, and *Unreal, Banana Peel!* — and Heather Russell's collection of children's playground games, *Carmen Out to Play!* As with these books, the original material for **Snug As A Bug!** is now housed in the Australian Children's Folklore Collection at the University of Melbourne.

Some of the items in **Snug As A Bug!**, like the magical 'wigwam for a goose's bridle', are centuries old and are part of our strong British heritage. Others have come from languages other than English, as spoken in Australia, and appear here in translation. The battle of wills between adults and children and the love of a good joke or a witty turn of phrase seem to know no ethnic boundaries. The index at the back of this book shows which original language each item comes from: all are from English unless otherwise indicated.

Readers of **Snug As A Bug!** are invited to write to me care of Oxford University Press, GPO Box 2784Y, Melbourne, 3001, with their own favourite family sayings. Perhaps there will soon be enough for another book!

Gwenda Beed Davey

TEA-TIME

What's for tea?

Possums' tossles and lambs' tails.

I'm as full as a goog.

Eat your dinner! Don't you know that an army marches on its stomach?

Waste not, want not,
For you may live to say
Oh how I wish I had the brussel sprouts
That once I threw away.

What's for tea, Mum?

An apple a day keeps the doctor away.

Snags, snags
Are mystery bags.

Your hair looks like a birch broom in a fit.

Mum's got eyes in the back of her head.

What's for tea, Mum?

Bread and butter and a duck under the table.

You're as slow as a wet week.

I'm tired!

Hi, tired, I'm Peter!

There was a pretty house,
Without a kitchen floor,
Without a roof,
Without a path,
Without a back door.
You couldn't go to bed,
You couldn't sleep a lot,
You couldn't even do pee-pee,
Because there was no pot.

Rabbit hot, rabbit cold,
Rabbit young, rabbit old,
Rabbit tender, rabbit tough,
Thanks be to God
I've had enough.

There was a little girl
And she had a little curl,
Right in the middle of her forehead.
And when she was good
She was very very good,
And when she was bad
She was horrid.

Empty vessels make the most sound.

Children should be seen and not heard.

What's for tea? My liver and kidneys.

Don't open your mouth and you won't catch any flies.

What's for tea?

Feathers — for a light meal.

Jack Sprat
Could eat no fat,
His wife could eat no lean,
And so between them both you see
They licked the platter clean.

What's for tea?
Pig's bum and gooligum.
NO
MEALS AT ALL HOURS
—BUT COME EARLY.
MENU

Half a pound of tuppeny rice,
Half a pound of treacle,
Put them together
And what have you got?
Pop goes the weasel!

All around the cobbler's bench,
The monkey chased the weasel,
The monkey stopped to pull up his socks,
Pop goes the weasel!

What's for tea? Wombat toes on toast.

Don't count your chickens until they're hatched.

There was an old woman
Who lived in a shoe,
She had so many children
She didn't know what to do.
She gave them some broth
Without any bread,
Then whipped them all soundly
And sent them to bed.

Don't get your knickers in a knot.

What's for tea?

Magpie stew.

One two three
Mother caught a flea
Put it in a teapot
And made a cup of tea.
Flea jumped out
Mother gave a shout
And in came Daddy
With his shirt
Hanging out.

What's for tea? Rocks.

Once I had a cat,
Her name was Katerina,
She wouldn't eat potatoes,
Or soup or semolina.
She wouldn't sing,
She wouldn't dance,
So I sent her off to Athens,
And then to France.

What's for tea?

Wind soup.

I'll have your guts for garters.

Rub a dub dub
Three men in a tub
And who do you think they were?
The butcher, the baker,
The candlestick maker,
They all ran after
A rotten potater.

How old are you?

Old enough to know best.

There was an old woman who swallowed a fly,
I don't know why she swallowed a fly.
I think she'll die.

There was an old woman who swallowed a spider,
Which wriggled and wriggled and jiggled inside her,
She swallowed the spider
To catch the fly,
I don't know why
She swallowed the fly.
I think she'll die.

There was an old woman who swallowed a bird,
How absurd to swallow a bird,
She swallowed the bird
To catch the spider
Which wriggled and wriggled and jiggled inside her,
She swallowed the spider
To catch the fly,
I don't know why
She swallowed the fly.
I think she'll die.

There was an old woman who swallowed a cat,
Just fancy that, to swallow a cat,
She swallowed the cat
To catch the bird,
How absurd to swallow a bird,
She swallowed the bird
To catch the spider
Which wriggled and wriggled and jiggled inside her,
She swallowed the spider
To catch the fly,
I don't know why
She swallowed the fly.
I think she'll die.

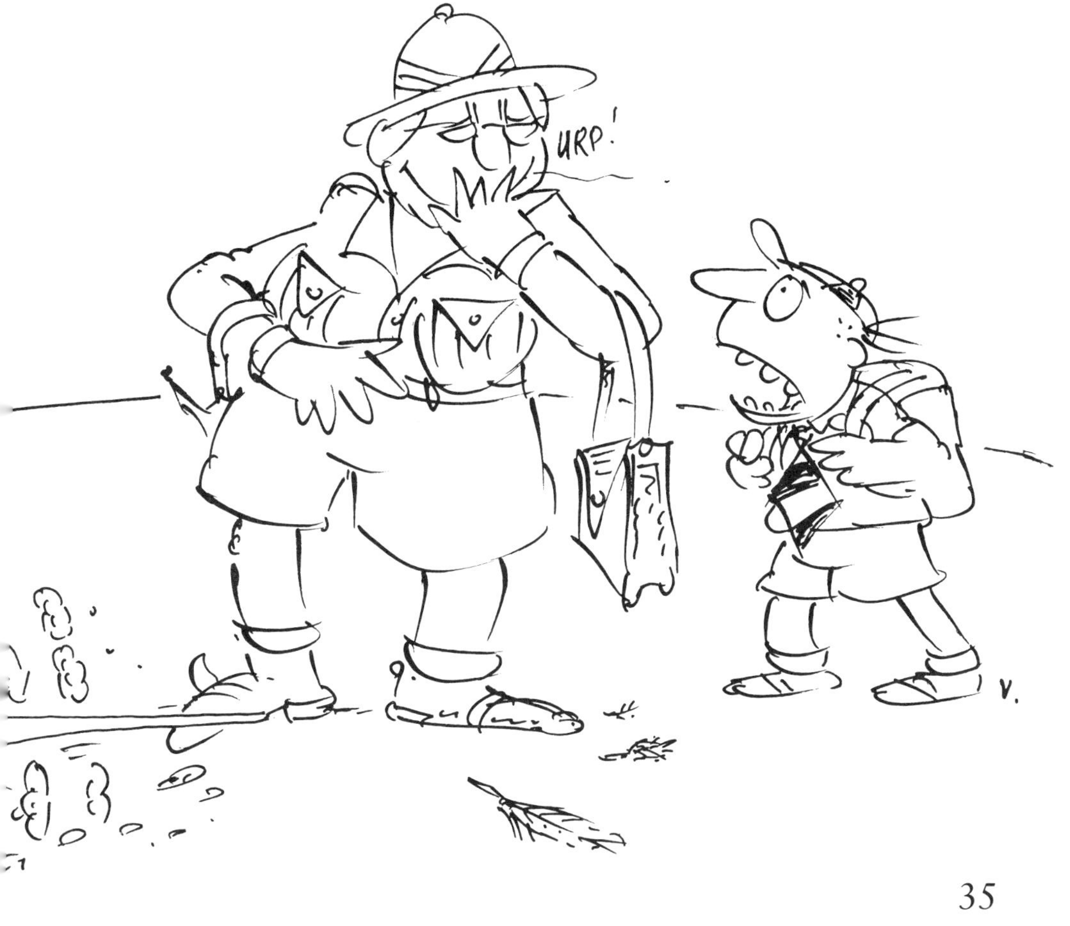
URP!
V.

There was an old woman who swallowed a dog,
Oh what a hog, to swallow a dog,
She swallowed the dog
To catch the cat,
Just fancy that, to swallow a cat,
She swallowed the cat
To catch the bird,
How absurd to swallow a bird,
She swallowed the bird
To catch the spider
Which wriggled and wriggled and jiggled inside her,
She swallowed the spider
To catch the fly,
I don't know why
She swallowed the fly,
I think she'll die.

37

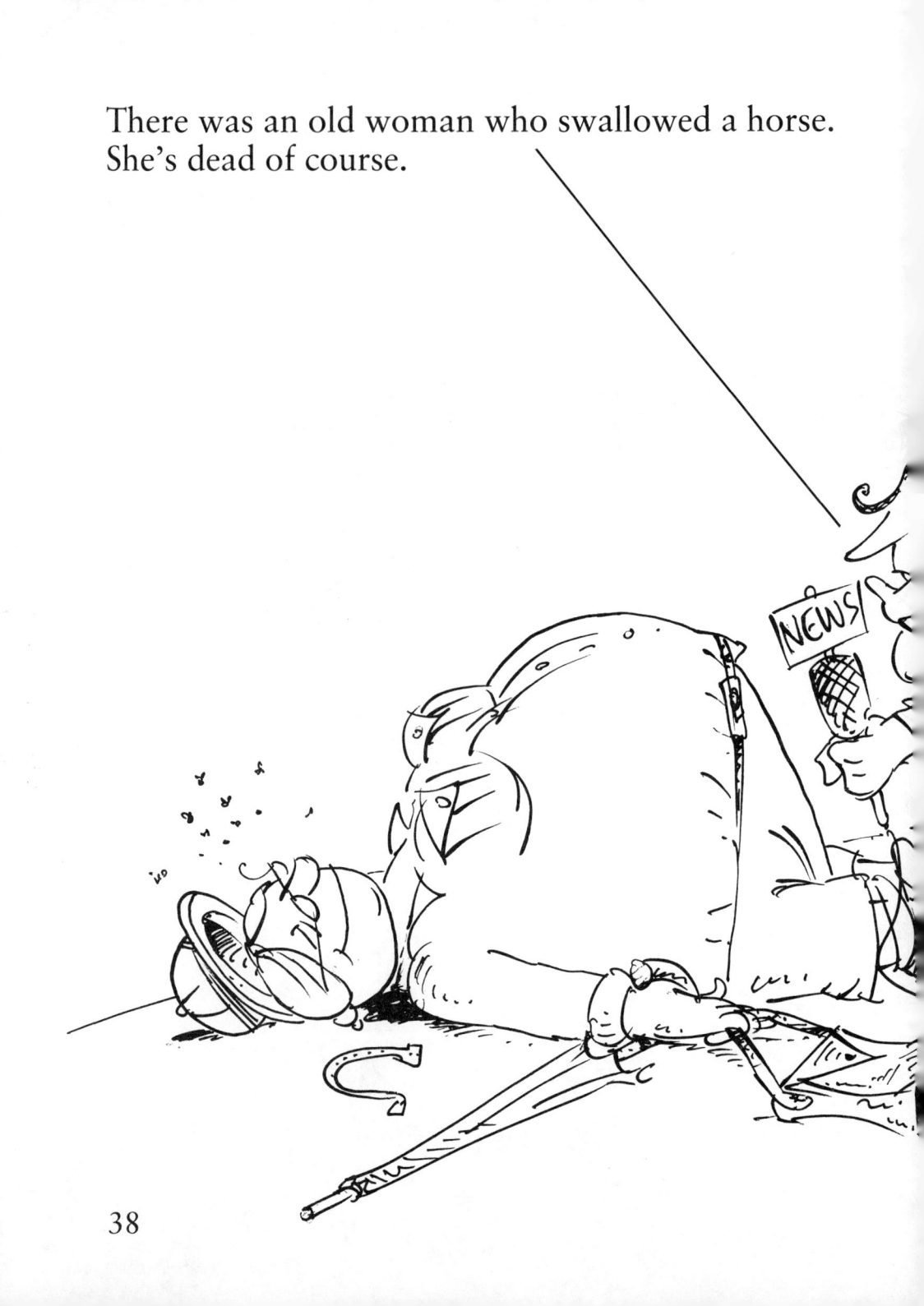

There was an old woman who swallowed a horse.
She's dead of course.

Your eyes are too big for your belly.

Eat your crusts. They'll make your hair curly.

CURIOSITY

How old are you, Mum?

As old as my tongue and as young as my teeth.

How old are you, Nanny?

About that, and maybe a little bit more.

How old are you, Dad?

Thirty-four going on twelve.

Where are you going?

To see a man about a dog.

What are you doing?

That's for me to know and you to find out.

What are you making?

A wigwam for a goose's bridle.

What are you doing?

Looking beautiful.

What'll I wear?

Wear your birthday suit.

What'll I do now?

Fart in a bottle and paint it blue.

What time is it?

Time you weren't here.

Where are you going, Dad?

There and back to see how far it is.

What'll I wear?

Wear your underpants back to front.

Where are we going?

Up the bum of a big black chook

What time is it?

Half past a freckle going on for a wart.

Why can't I?

'Cause Y is a crooked letter and you can't make it straight.

What?

He invented the steam engine.

How old are you, Grandpa?

As old as the sun and as young as the sea.

Well?

Where's the well?

Where are you going?

What's the time?

Where are you going?

I'm going to the mountains for some monkeys.

Half past nine: hang your britches on the line.

Up the wall if you don't stop asking me.

Watch out, it'll bite you if you come any closer.

What's for tea, Mum?

How long will tea be?

Fried frogs' legs.

About three feet.

Mum, where are my socks?

Up in Nanna's room hanging on a hook.

Where are you going?

To Timbuctoo.

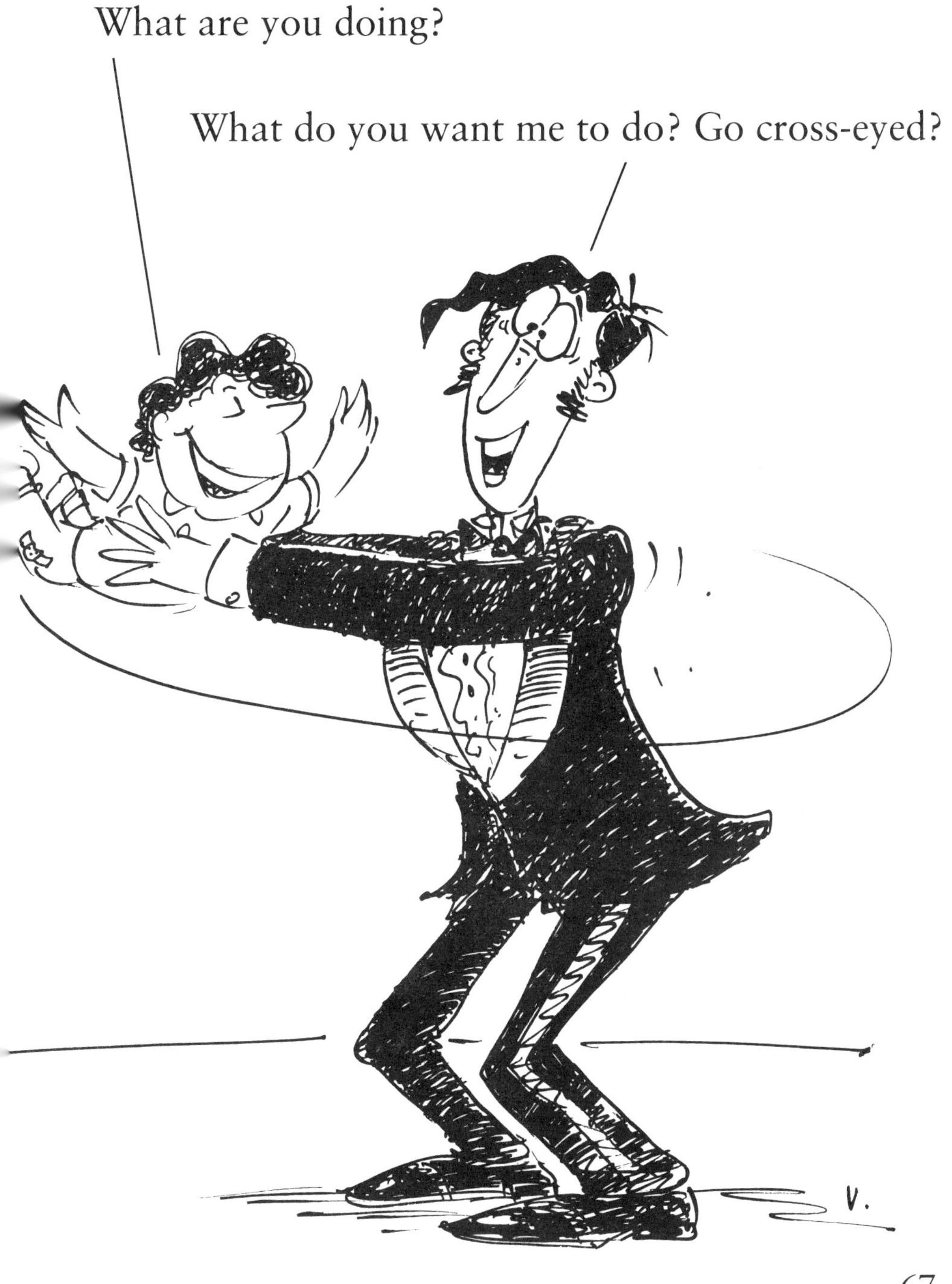
What are you doing?
What do you want me to do? Go cross-eyed?

How old are you?

Twenty-five years per leg.

SILLY SAYINGS

Little pigs have big ears.

She's the cat's mother.

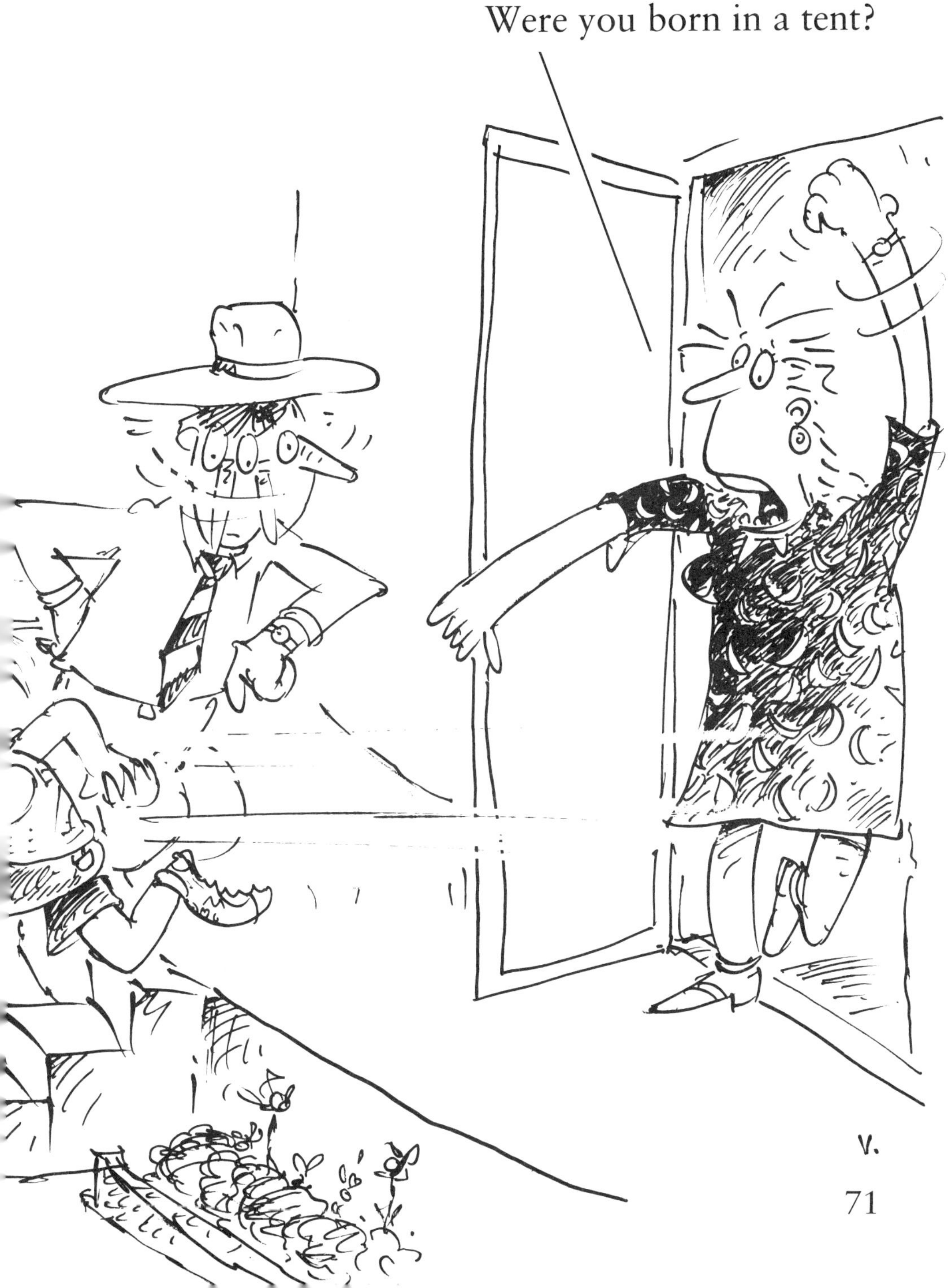
Were you born in a tent?

You'd talk the leg off an iron pot!

All work and no play
Makes Jack a dull boy.

My ears are burning.

Get a wriggle on!

Quick sticks! Somebody's talking about you.

Rattle your dags!

Giddy giddy gout
Your shirt's hanging out,
Ten miles in
And ten miles out.

You're as silly as a wet hen.

Ay?

Bee. Watch out it doesn't sting you.

It's no use crying over spilt milk.

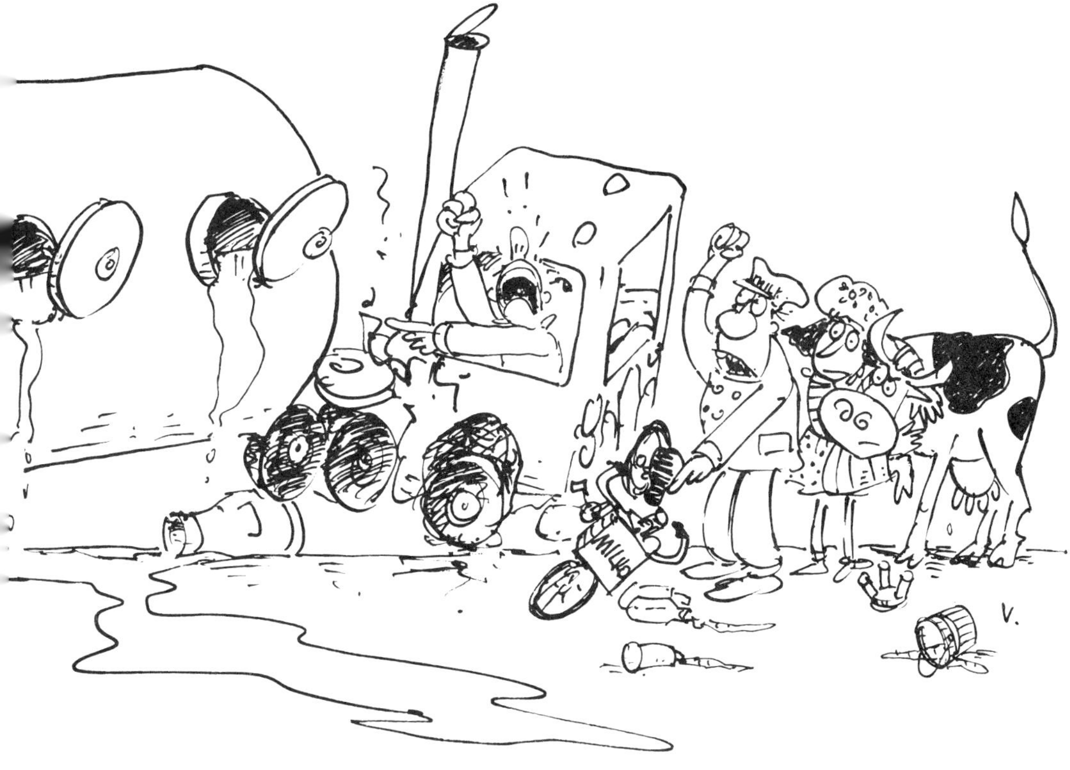
MILK
MILKO
V.

Ups a daisy!

Look before you leap!

A stitch in time saves nine.

Pull your socks up!

IFs & DON'Ts

If you cry on your birthday, you'll cry all the year.

Don't point —
you'll put holes in the air and the fairies will fall out.

If you don't shut up
I'll drop you like a sparrer in the Yarra.

Don't be a bossy britches.

If you say that again,
I'll wash your mouth out with soap.

Don't be a Whingeing Willie.

If you watch too much TV, you'll get square eyes.

Don't get off your bike: I'll pick up your pump.

If you don't hurry up,
Christmas will get here first.

Don't care.

Don't care was made to care
Don't care was hung,
Don't care was put in a pot
And made to hold his tongue.

If the wind changes while you're pulling a face, you'll stay that way.

If you don't wash your ears, potatoes will grow out of them.

If at first you don't succeed, try, try, try again.

BED-TIME

Early to bed, early to rise
Makes you healthy, wealthy and wise.

I'll tell you a story
About Jack-a-Nory.
Shall I begin it?
That's all that's in it.

To bed to bed said Sleepyhead,
Half a mo said Slow.
Put on the pot,
Said Greedy Gut,
We'll have some tea before we go.

Good night, God bless,
May the fleas undress,
And the bugs run away
With your clothes.

Red sky at night
A sailor's delight.
Red sky in the morning
A sailor's warning.

Snug as a bug in a rug!

Index

A stitch in time   82
All work and no play   73
An apple a day   6
Ay? Bee   79
Children should be seen   13
Don't be a bossy britches   87
Don't be a Whingeing Willie   89
Don't care was made to care   93
Don't count your chickens   21
Don't get off your bike   91
Don't get your knickers in a knot   23
Don't open your mouth   15
Don't point   85
Early to bed   98
Eat your crusts   40
Eat your dinner   5
Empty vessels   12
Eyes in the back of her head   7
Full as a goog   4
Get a wriggle on   74
Giddy giddy gout   76
Good night, God bless   101
Half a pound of tuppeny rice   19
How long will tea be? About three feet   63
How old are you?
    About that   43
    As old as my tongue   42
    As old as the sun   58
    Old enough to know best   30
    Thirty-four   44
    Twenty-five years per leg (Italian)   68
If at first you don't succeed   96
If the wind changes   94
If you cry on your birthday   84
If you don't hurry up   92
If you don't shut up   86
If you don't wash your ears   95

If you say that again   88
If you watch too much TV   90
I'll have your guts for garters   28
I'll tell you a story   99
I'm tired   8
It's no use crying   80

Jack Sprat   17

Little pigs have big ears   70
Look before you leap   82

My ears are burning   74

Once I had a cat (Greek)   27
One two three, mother caught a flea   25

Pull your socks up   82

Quick sticks   75

Rabbit hot, rabbit cold   10
Rattle your dags   75
Red sky at night   102
Rub a dub dub, three men in a tub   29

She's the cat's mother   70
Snags, snags   6
Snug as a bug in a rug   103

There was a little girl   11
There was an old woman who lived in a shoe   22
There was an old woman who swallowed a fly   31–38
There was a pretty house (Italian)   9
To bed, to bed, said Sleepyhead   100

Ups a daisy   82

Waste not want not   5
Watch out, it'll bite you   62
Well? Where's the well?   59
Were you born in a tent?   71
What time is it? Time you weren't here   51
What are you doing?
    Looking beautiful   48
      That's for me to know   46
        What do you want me to do? (Greek)   67
What are you making? A wigwam   47
What? He invented the steam engine   57

What time is it? Half past a freckle   55
What'll I do now? Fart in a bottle   50
What'll I wear?
    Your birthday suit   49
    Your underpants   53
What's for tea?
    Bread and butter   8
    Feathers   16
    Fried frog's legs   63
    Magpie stew   24
    My liver and kidneys (Greek)   14
    Pig's bum and gooligum   18
    Possum's tossles and lambs' tails   4
    Rocks (Greek)   26
    Wind soup   28
    Wombat toes on toast   20
What's the time?
    Half past nine   61
    Time you weren't here   51
Where are my socks? Up in Nanna's room   65
Where are you going?
    There and back   52
    To see a man   45
    To Timbuctoo   66
    To the mountains   61
    Up the wall (Italian)   61
Where are we going? Up the bum of a big black chook   54
Why can't I? Because Y's a crooked letter   56

You'd talk the leg off an iron pot   72
You're as silly as a wet hen   77
You're as slow as a wet week   8
Your eyes are too big   39
Your hair looks like a birch broom   7

About the author

Gwenda Beed Davey is a respected authority on Australian folklore and has lectured in Australian Folklore Studies at the Institute for Early Childhood Development and elsewhere. She traces her interest in household sayings back to her own childhood when her grandmother would complain of 'having a bone in her leg', and her father would say he was 'going to see a man about a dog'.

About the illustrator

Peter Viska is a well-known and much-loved animator and illustrator, mainly of children's books. His other projects include designing and illustrating stamps for the Australian Bicentenary and the International Year of Literacy. Some of his earliest influences as an illustrator, he says, were the cartoons of *MAD* magazine. Peter's fans will agree that beneath the cheeky deftness of his drawings is a keen understanding of children and their world. These qualities have brought to life the popular collections of children's sayings, rhymes and games published by Oxford University Press.